Daniel in the Lions' Den

First box set edition, 2015

Sky Pony Press books may be purchased in bulk at special discounts for sales promotion, corporate gifts, fund-raising, or educational purposes. Special editions can also be created to specifications. For details, contact the Special Sales Department, Sky Pony Press, 307 West 36th Street, 11th Floor, New York, NY 10018 or info@skyhorsepublishing.com.

Sky Pony® is a registered trademark of Skyhorse Publishing, Inc.®, a Delaware corporation.

Visit our website at www.skyponypress.com.

10 9 8 7 6 5 4 3 2 1

Manufactured in China, May 2015
This product conforms to CPSIA 2008

Library of Congress has cataloged the hardcover trade edition as follows:

Smith, Brendan Powell, author.
Daniel in the lions' den : the brick Bible for kids / Brendan Powell Smith.
pages cm. -- (The brick Bible for kids)
Summary: "The story of Daniel being thrown into the lions' den as illustrated with LEGO bricks."-- Provided by publisher.
Audience: Ages 3-6.
Audience: Pre-school.
ISBN 978-1-62914-605-8 (hardcover : alk. paper) 1. Daniel (Biblical figure)--Juvenile literature. 2. Bible stories, English--Daniel. 3. LEGO toys--Juvenile literature. I. Title.
BS580.D2S58 2014
224.509505--dc23
2014002886

Cover design by Brian Peterson
Cover photo credit Brendan Powell Smith

Slipcase ISBN: 978-1-63450-208-5
Ebook ISBN: 978-1-63220-205-5

Editor: Julie Matysik
Designer: Brian Peterson
Production Manager: Sara Kitchen

Daniel in the Lions' Den
THE BRICK BIBLE for Kids

Brendan Powell Smith

Sky Pony Press
New York

King Nebuchadnezzar and his army conquered Israel where God's people, the Israelites, lived. Then he took all the Israelites with him back to the city of Babylon where his people had a different religion. One of the Israelites who was taken to Babylon was a young boy named Daniel.

Daniel and his three friends from Israel were smart, good-looking boys. The king put them in a special school so they would grow up to be very wise and would help the king rule over his enormous kingdom. With God's help, Daniel and his friends became very wise indeed.

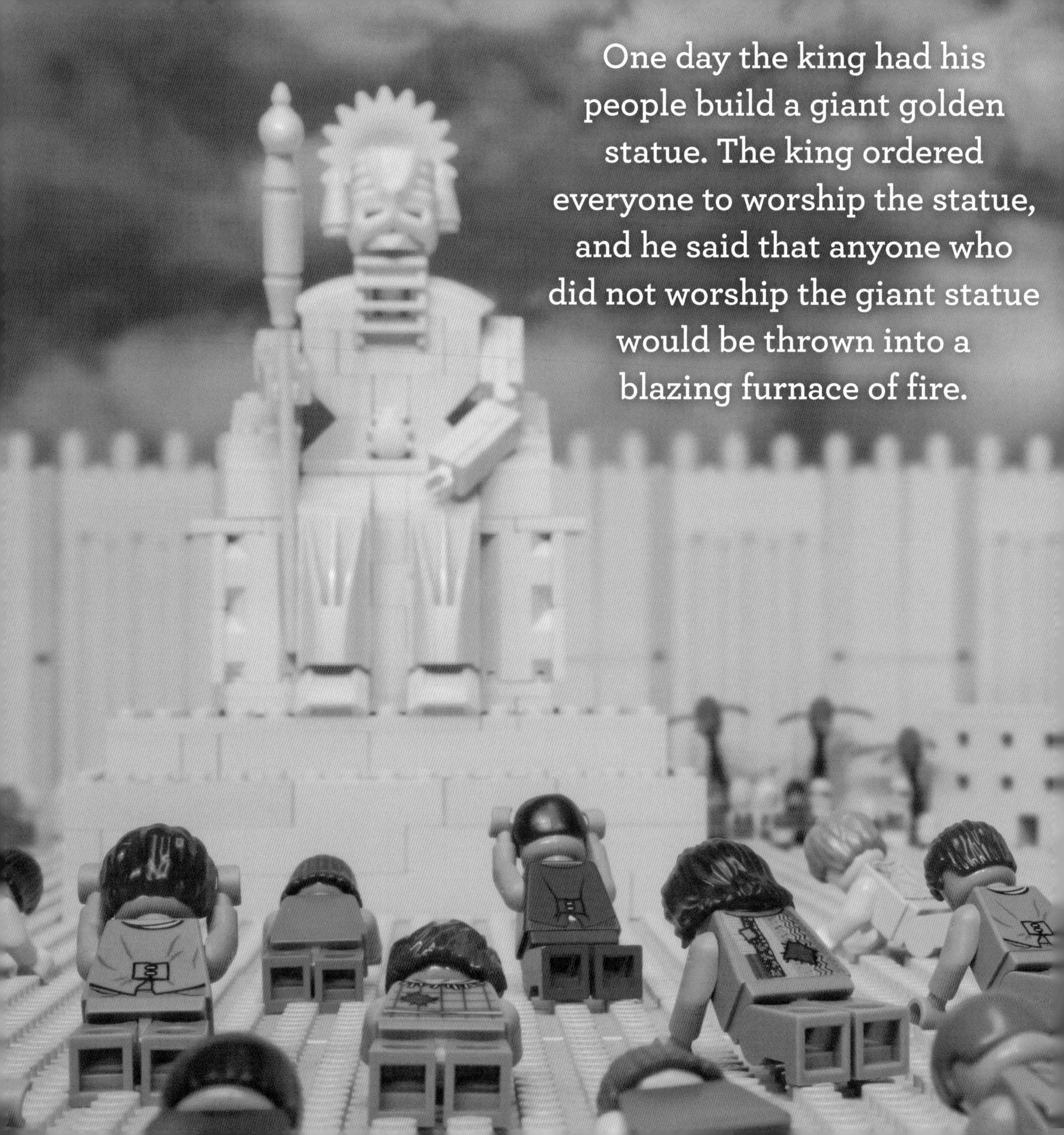
One day the king had his
people build a giant golden
statue. The king ordered
everyone to worship the statue,
and he said that anyone who
did not worship the giant statue
would be thrown into a
blazing furnace of fire.

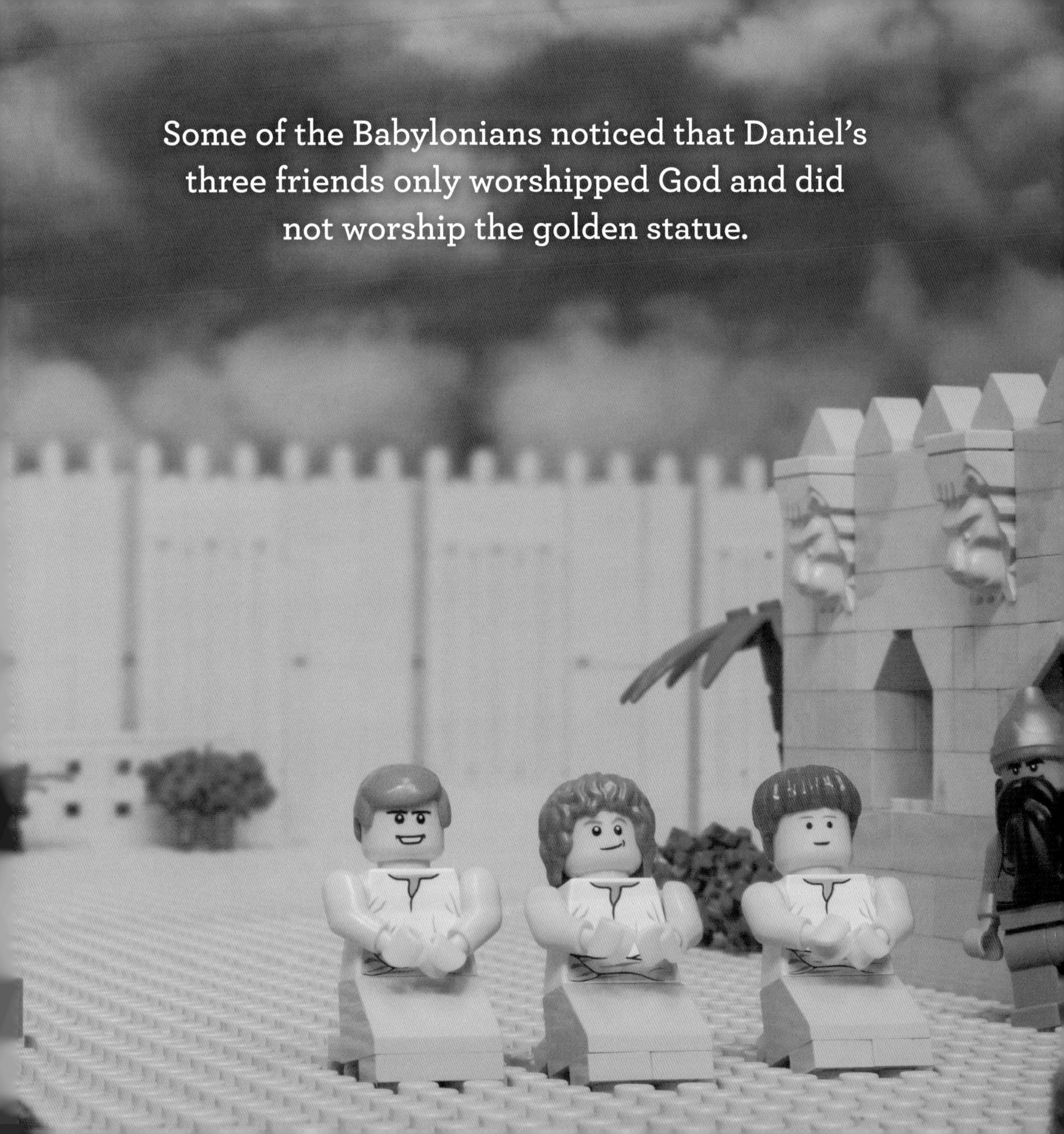

Some of the Babylonians noticed that Daniel's three friends only worshipped God and did not worship the golden statue.

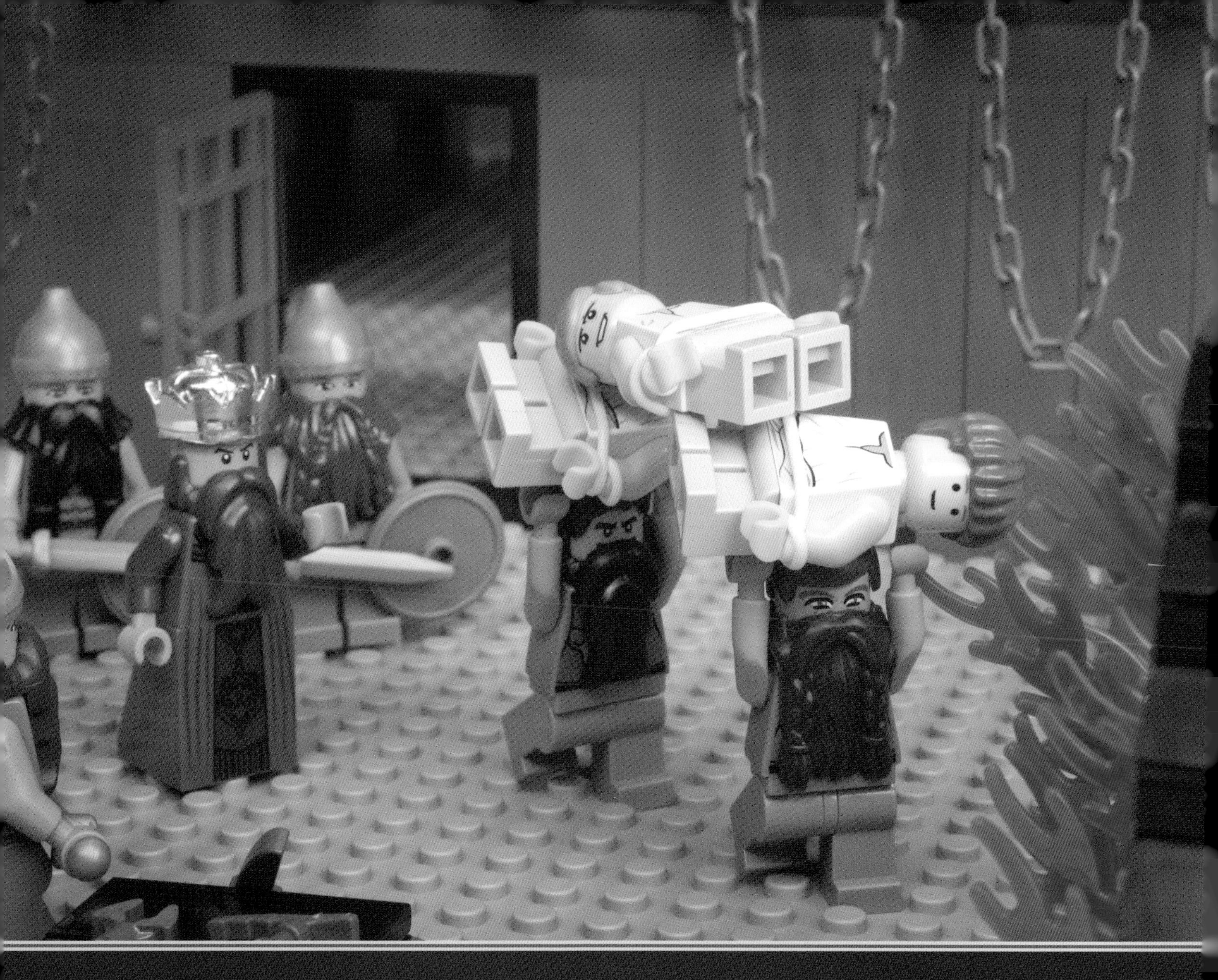

When the king found out, he became very angry. He had Daniel's three friends tied up and ordered two of his strongest soldiers to lift up the three friends and toss them into the blazing furnace.

The fire in the furnace was so hot that flames were leaping out. As Daniel's three friends were tossed into the furnace, the two soldiers caught on fire and were burned up.

Daniel's friends stood inside the blazing furnace, but they were not harmed. As the king looked on, he noticed a fourth figure had joined them amid the flames. He saw that it was an angel sent by God to protect Daniel's three friends.

The king ordered the three friends to come out of the fire, and he was amazed to see they had not been harmed. The king gained respect for their God and he made this announcement to his people: "Anyone who says anything bad about the God of the Israelites will be put to death."

One day, the king woke up from a frightening dream. In the dream he saw a very tall tree. There were birds living in the tree, and there were wild animals living below the tree in its shade. Then an angel appeared and announced that the tree would be cut down.

The king gathered his wise men and told them the dream, but no one could tell him what it meant. Finally, the king told the dream to Daniel. Daniel knew what the dream meant, but was afraid to tell the king. The king insisted.

So Daniel told the king its meaning. "You have grown very big and strong, like the tree in your dream," said Daniel. "But God has decided that you will be humbled for a time and live among the wild animals."

And so it happened one day that the king was walking along the roof of his royal palace, admiring the view of the city. "Here is the great city of Babylon," he said, "which has been built by my mighty strength for my honor and glory."

At that very moment, the king suddenly found himself among the wild animals, far away from any cities or towns. He lived like an animal for some time, eating grass and sleeping outdoors. His hair grew long, and his fingernails grew into claws.

After some time passed, God returned him to his place as king of Babylon and made him more powerful than before. The king had learned to be humble before the God of Israel. He praised God and marveled at God's power over all humans.

Many years later the king's son became the new king of Babylon. At a great feast for his friends, the new king served wine in golden cups that had been taken from the Temple of the God of the Israelites. During the meal, the Babylonians gave praise to the gods of their religion.

Suddenly the king saw a human hand appear out of nowhere and it began writing something on the wall nearby. The king turned white with fear, and his guests were scared and confused. When the writing was complete, the hand vanished.

The new king gathered all his wise men to read the writing on the wall, but none of them could figure out what it said or what it meant.

Then the queen remembered that many years ago, Daniel had once helped the king's father by telling him what his frightening dream had meant. So Daniel was found and brought to the new king to help him.

Daniel could read the writing on the wall and he knew its meaning. He said to the king, "The message says that you have failed to respect the God of Israel and that God will now bring an end to your rule." That very night, the new king was killed.

The next king was named Darius. He chose several assistants to help him rule over his kingdom. Since Daniel was most skilled, the king put him in charge of all his assistants. This made the other assistants jealous of Daniel, and they made a plan to get rid of him.

To get Daniel in trouble, the other assistants convinced King Darius to make a new law. It said that for the next thirty days, if anyone worships anyone other than the king of Babylon, they will be thrown into a den of lions.

Daniel knew about the new law, but continued to worship the God of Israel. So the king's assistants came to Daniel's house and saw him worshipping his God. They told the king about this and reminded him that Daniel must be thrown into a den of lions.

King Darius liked Daniel and did not want to hurt him, but he knew he must do what the new law required. So the king had Daniel thrown into a den of lions, and said to him, "Maybe the God that you always worship will save you from the lions!"

A large stone was rolled over the opening of the lions' den so Daniel could not escape. That night King Darius was so worried about Daniel that he could not eat any food and did not get any sleep.

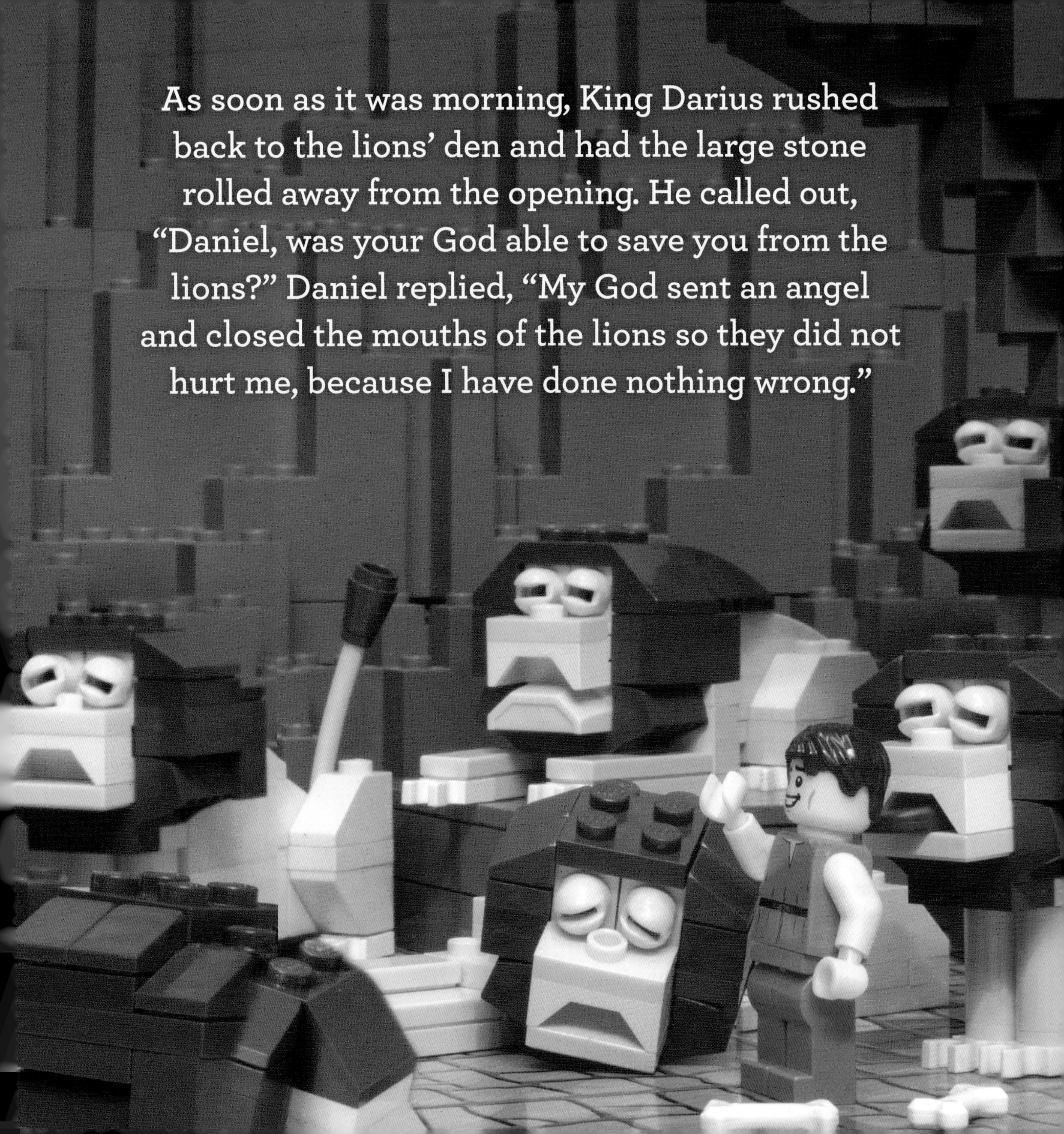

As soon as it was morning, King Darius rushed back to the lions' den and had the large stone rolled away from the opening. He called out, "Daniel, was your God able to save you from the lions?" Daniel replied, "My God sent an angel and closed the mouths of the lions so they did not hurt me, because I have done nothing wrong."

King Darius was amazed. He had Daniel taken up out of the lions' den. Then he ordered the assistants who tried to get rid of Daniel to be thrown into the lions' den with their wives and children. The lions tore them all apart before they even reached the ground.

The king then announced that all the people in the world should shake with fear before the God of the Israelites who rules over the world forever and who saved Daniel from the jaws of the lions.

Activity!

Can you find these ten brick pieces in the book?
On which page does each appear?
The answers are below.

A.

B.

C.

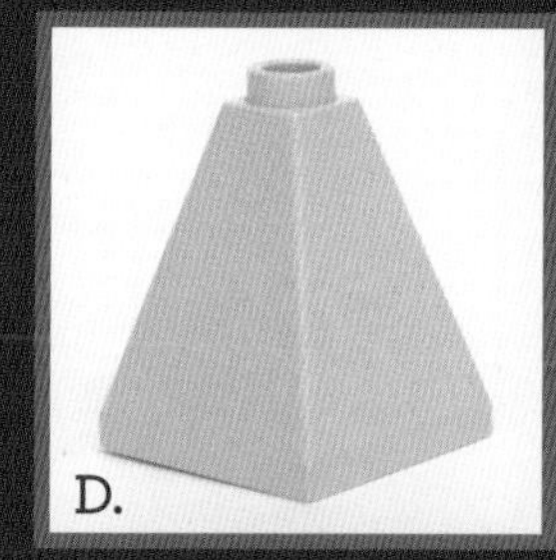
D.

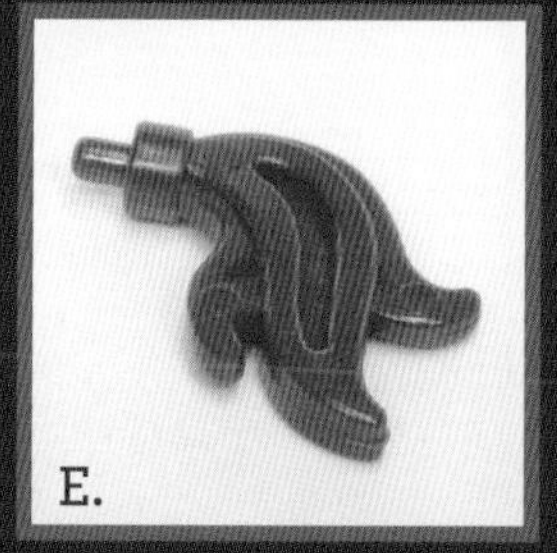
E.

F.

G.

H.

I.

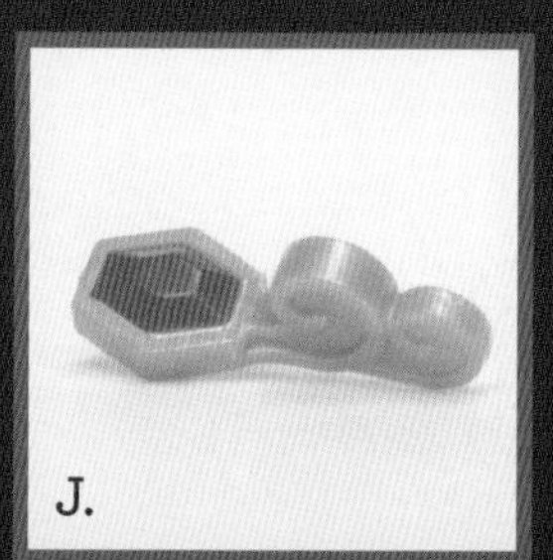
J.

Answer key:

A: p. 25, B: p. 7, C: p. 31, D: p. 15, E: p. 20, F: p. 6, G: p. 24, H: p. 5, I: p. 12, J: p. 13.